The whisper of a fairy
The magic of its word
Will help those in the forest
Whenever it is heard

And when there is danger
Wherever there is need
A fairy's care and help
Will be there indeed

a min@dition book
published by Penguin Young Readers Group

Text copyright © 2008 by Simone Lindner
Illustrations copyright © 2008 by Christa Unzner
Original title: Wasserelfe Aelin
English text translation by Kathryn Bishop
Coproduction with Michael Neugebauer Publishing Ltd., Hong Kong.
Licensed by Margarete Steiff GmbH, Giengen, Germany
Rights arranged with "minedition" Rights and Licensing AG, Zurich, Switzerland.
Published simultaneously in Canada.
Manufactured in Hong Kong by Wide World Ltd.
Typesetting in Frutiger, by Adrian Frutiger.
Color separation by Fotoriproduzione Grafiche, Verona, Italy.

Library of Congress Cataloging-in-Publication Data available upon request.

ISBN 978-0-698-40072-6

10 9 8 7 6 5 4 3 2 1
First Impression

For more information please visit our website: www.minedition.com

Also published in this series:

Aelin, the Water Fairy
Runya, the Fire Fairy
Tara, the Air Fairy

Amar, the Earth Fairy

by Simone Lindner
Illustrated by Christa Unzner
Translated by Kathryn Bishop

minedition

Amar, the little Earth Fairy, sat rubbing his belly.
"If I eat even one more," he said, "I'll surely pop."
But he looked longingly at all the other apples.
He opened the top button of his trousers and thought
about taking a nice nap.
"Perhaps it would be better if I took a walk in the forest."
He got up, adjusted his boots, and slipped into his
grass-green invisibility cloak.

Soon the Earth Fairy was scampering on his way, skipping from one patch of moss to the next.

With each jump, seeds sprinkled from his pockets and blossomed into tiny flowers.

As he walked along, Amar saw a large, important-looking black beetle sitting on a blade of grass. He just couldn't resist. He pulled the blade of grass downward, and when he let it go, he sent the fat beetle flying.

"Hey! What a naughty little fairy you are!" yelled the beetle as he went whirling by.

But Amar skipped on, laughing merrily.

Suddenly the Earth Fairy heard something.
He stopped and listened.
Was that someone crying? Amar crept closer
to get a better look. Sitting next to a freshly dug
molehill was a mole, weeping miserably.
Amar also noticed that not far away was a badger who looked
ready to gobble up the little mole. He had to do something.
He began reciting words from the world of magical beings.

Ni nalla tulu!
I call for help!

Heart of a fairy, brave and true
Show me now what I must do
The badger's hungry, I need a trick
To save the mole, I must be quick

"I've got it!" he said.

Amar ran quickly to the mole, whipped off his cloak, and threw it over his head. The badger was ready to pounce, but suddenly the mole had disappeared. There was nothing there but green grass. He looked and looked, but there was no trace of the mole. The fairy cloak had made him invisible. As Amar watched, the badger kept looking and sniffing. Finally, the disappointed animal ran back into the woods.

"Can I help you, little mole?" asked Amar, gently lifting the cloak.

The mole twitched nervously. He squinted and blinked in the bright sunlight with his shoe-button eyes. "Don't be afraid. It's only me, Amar, the Earth Fairy. Here's a soft leaf to dry your tears. Now, tell me why you're crying."

The mole blew his nose and brushed away his tears. "Have you lost your mother?" asked Amar.

"I ran away," answered the mole sadly. "My name is Coron, I wanted to see what it was like above ground. We've always lived underground, you know. But up here I can't see anything. It's too bright. And I cut my foot, and now it's bleeding. And I don't even know how to get home!"

And with that he started to cry again.

Amar patted him gently on the head.

"No mole sees very well when they're above ground, but they have great noses for smelling, and they are the very best diggers. Now, where does it hurt?" Amar asked.

The little mole stretched out his back leg. A sharp rock had made a deep cut in his foot.

"Oh my, oh my...yes, that must really hurt!" said Amar. "But we're lucky. Mother Nature has plants that can heal anything."

Amar stood up and began searching. He knew all the healing plants in the fields and woods, and was certain he could find just the right one.

"Here, ribwort. The green juice in the leaves helps swelling. And here, the arnica plant! It helps everything heal faster." Amar picked a few of the ribwort leaves and pressed them between his hands until they were soft and a green juice poured out. He spread the juice over the mole's foot, added some of the arnica blossoms, and bandaged him up with some leaves.

"Now we need something to help from the inside."
He pulled a yellow-gold candy from his cloak and stuck it in the mole's mouth.
"Here's some candy made from sage and sweet honey. It will help you…and it tastes good too! Now let's get you home."

The mole limped along with his bandaged foot, stopping once in a while to rub himself against a rock, some grass, or the ground.

"What are you doing?" Amar asked, confused.

"I am marking the way. It will smell like me, and my mother will know which way I am going."

"Have you at least found anything interesting up here above ground?" Amar asked.

Coron laughed and opened his hands. In one hand were two beautiful stones, and in the other an earthworm.

"What wonderful treasures. Your mother will surely be pleased," said Amar. "But we must hurry. I'm sure she is very worried and is looking for you everywhere!"

And Amar was right. Just as the two were about
to go on, the ground next to them started to move.
Suddenly a velvety black head appeared.
It was Mama Mole!

"Mama!" called the small mole as he happily fell into his mother's arms.

"Coron, where have you been?" his mother cried, kissing him on the nose and holding him tightly. "I should scold you, you know. But I am just so glad that you are all right."

"Well, almost," said Amar. Then he told her what had happened, and showed her which leaves she should use when changing the bandage.

"In a few days it will be good as new," he promised.

"But now it is time for my afternoon nap," said Amar.

Suddenly, the invisibility cloak magically lifted up into the air, floated through a cloud of meadow flowers, and slowly drifted back to the ground.

Amar looked up to the sky and saw a gleaming light, as bright as the midday sun, and he heard a gentle voice.

"Amar, you have done your job as Earth Fairy well."

"*Bereth*, the Fairy Queen," whispered Amar respectfully as he bowed deeply. The Queen glistened in her flowing white dress, sparkling with the light of a thousand diamonds. Her long hair shone, and her delicate wings shimmered with every color of the rainbow.

"Amar," she said.
"You are a special Earth Fairy.
  For a long time you have cared
  for the earth and rocks, the plants and
  the animals. I would now like
  to send you into the world
  of human children.
  Are you ready to go?"
  Amar was so excited
  His face lit up and he nodded happily.
"Yes, I'm ready."

  The Fairy Queen opened a little
  linen bag and took out a ring of gold.
"Amar, Earth Fairy, I hereby present to you
  the magic fairy ring,
  the ring of your element, earth."

"The ring will serve you in the human world.
It will help you exchange secret messages and it will
seal your friendships. When it is placed on the ground, it will
create a large circle, and only those who enter it will be able to
see you, to speak and dance with you. From now on you are
to be a friend and protector of a human child.
That child is reading this story
and is waiting for you."

Amar smiled and placed
the ring on his finger.

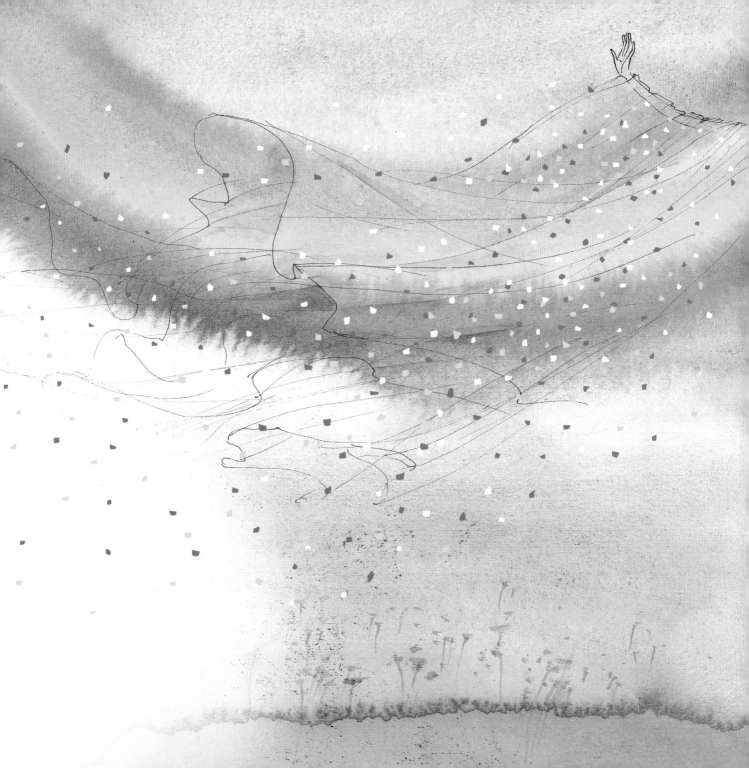

Then the shining light disappeared as suddenly as it had come.
For Amar, the Earth Fairy, a new adventure was about to begin...

Could his adventure be with *you?*

Which of the elements suits you best?

WATER and *Aelin*

1. imaginative
2. bubbly
3. creative
4. pure
5. lakes, rivers
6. sea, ocean
7. waves
8. waterfalls
9. raindrops, snowflakes
10. ice crystals
11. slide, float
12. swim

FIRE and *Runya*

1. fiery
2. warm-hearted
3. explosive
4. enthusiastic
5. full of energy
6. gives warmth
7. brings light in the darkness
8. sparkling
9. crackle
10. sun
11. fire light
12. firesides

EARTH and *Amar* ◯

1. rascal
2. steadfast
3. healing abilities
4. good-natured
5. rocks and stones
6. mountains and valley
7. forests and meadows
8. earth, trees, and roots
9. plants and flowers
10. digging
11. playing in the sand
12. all 4 seasons

Air and *Tara*

1. happy
2. playful
3. quick-tempered
4. wind
5. storm
6. sky
7. clouds
8. flying with birds
9. soaring, floating
10. feeling free as a breeze
11. feeling light as a feather
12. pinwheels and kites

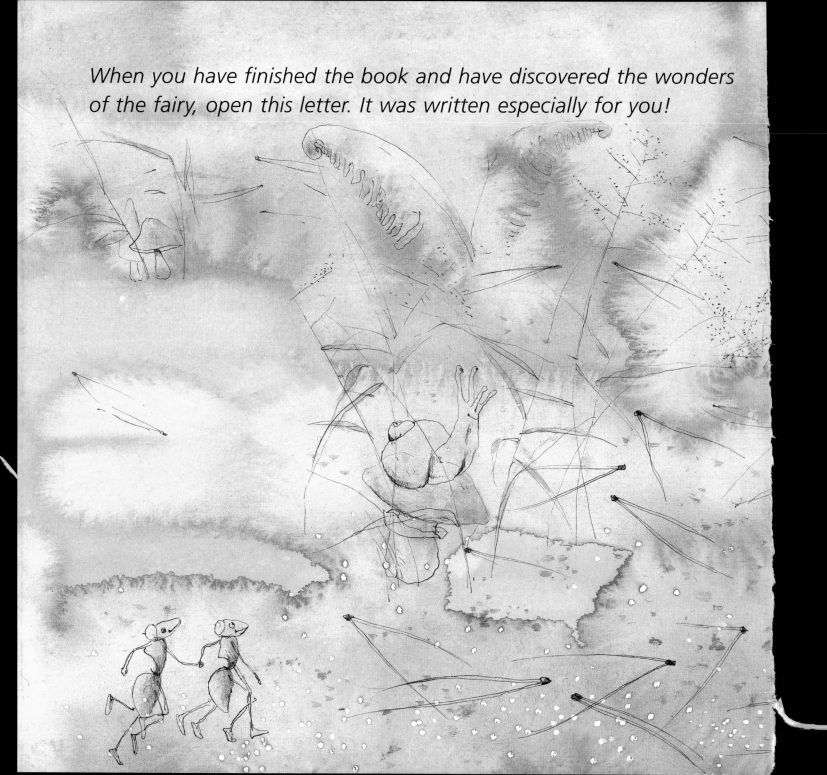

When you have finished the book and have discovered the wonders of the fairy, open this letter. It was written especially for you!